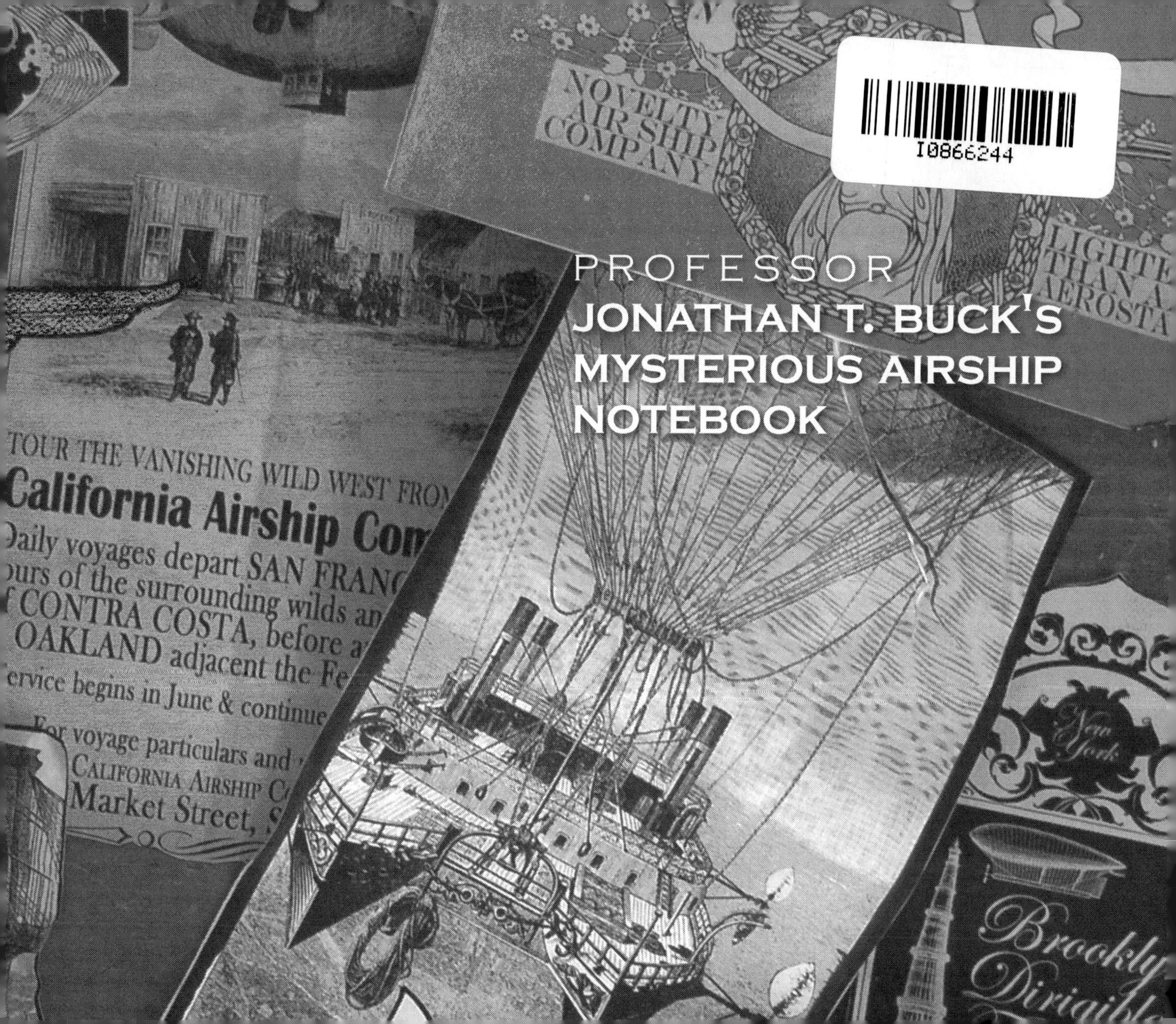

PROFESSOR JONATHAN T. BUCK'S MYSTERIOUS AIRSHIP NOTEBOOK

FIRST
DISCOVER
THE
IRWIN BROS.
GEARS
KNOBS
Barnes Steam Machines
B

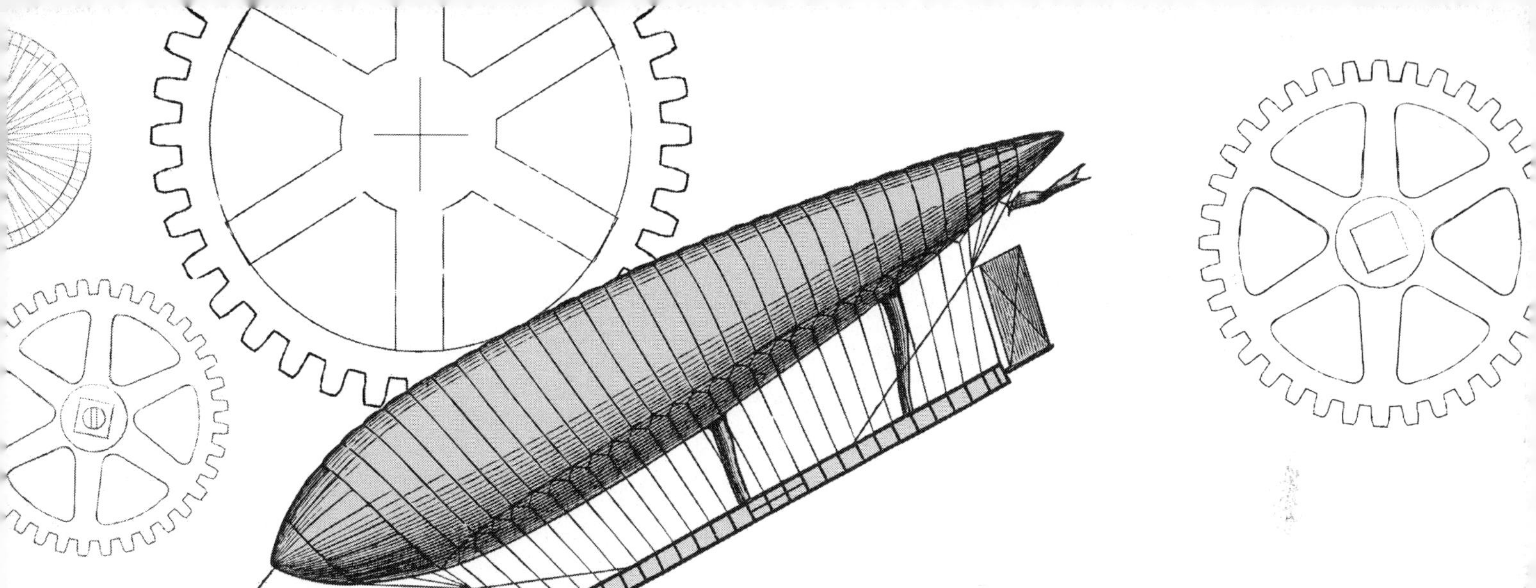

PROFESSOR

JONATHAN T. BUCK'S MYSTERIOUS AIRSHIP NOTEBOOK

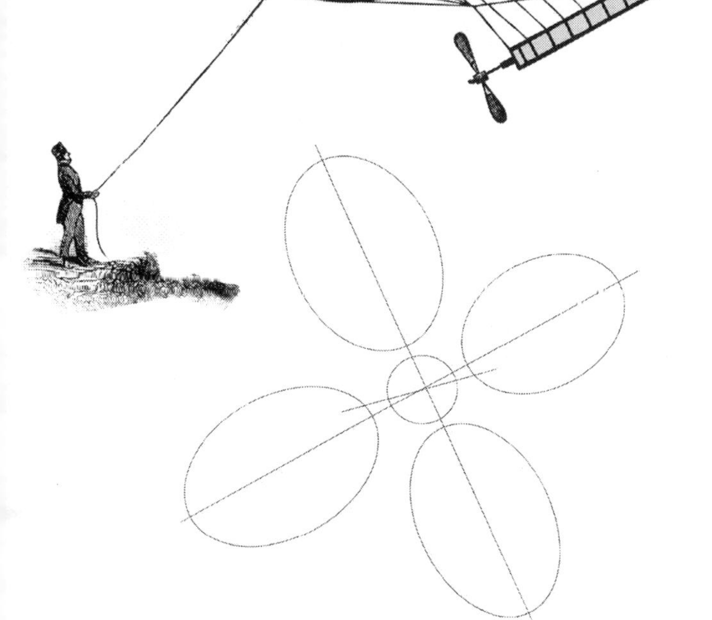

The Lost Step-by-Step Dirigible Drawings from the Pioneer of Steampunk Design

BY KEITH RIEGERT & SAMUEL KAPLAN
ILLUSTRATED BY JONATHAN BUCK

ULYSSES PRESS

Published by:
Ulysses Press
PO Box 3440
Berkeley, CA 94703
www.ulyssespress.com

ISBN: 978-1-64604-299-9
Library of Congress Control Number: 2012937117

Printed in the United States

10 9 8 7 6 5 4 3 2 1

Acquisitions editor: Keith Riegert
Design and layout: Jenna Stempel
Production: Jake Flaherty
Cover artwork: © Jonathan Buck; © Morphart Creations/Shutterstock.com; © Dover Publishing; © Antonio Abrignani/Shutterstock.com; © Slava Gerj/Shutterstock.com
Interior artwork: see page 37

Contents

APS Claire *photographed over New Orleans during its four-hour maiden voyage, 1887.*

Foreword: The Man Beneath the Balloon

JONATHAN T. BUCK

BORN: BATON ROUGE, LOUISIANA,
SEPTEMBER 17, 1850; DIED: UNKNOWN

Jonathan T. Buck was an American engineer, riverboat captain, flight pioneer, and esteemed adventurer. Considered one of the great innovators of controlled aeronautical flight, he is most famous for designing and constructing the **Air Paddle Steamer *Claire***, an elegant steam-powered riverboat dirigible, which was fully navigable through sky and, if necessary, water. Professor Buck's historic air voyage took the *Claire* nearly 2,500 miles through the Amazon rainforest in search of the mysterious lost city of Madeira before Buck, his crew, and the *Claire* disappeared into the hot, dense jungles of the southern Amazon, never to be seen again.

Final newspaper portrait of Buck just before the Madeira Expedition (January 1888).

A GIFTED BOAT BUILDER

The son of a renowned steamboat builder, Buck learned the trade firsthand, captaining his own Mississippi riverboat at the age of 15 and then becoming a bright and gifted apprentice nautical engineer. As an engineer, Buck was truly brilliant—by the age of 20 he had patented two dozen designs, ranging from miniature steam boilers, propellers, and internal combustion engines to a lightweight alloy known as "Buck's iron."

INTO THE AMAZON

In 1871, 21-year-old Buck, yearning for adventure, signed on as chief engineer of the Amazonas Trading Company, a steamboat outfit running rubber trees out of the deep jungles of the Amazon. Stationed out of Iquitos, Peru, nearly 1,900 miles up the world's largest river, Buck often traveled from the headwaters to the Atlantic, diverting down dozens of snaking tributaries along the way, as he repaired boats and charted new routes. It was during these voyages through the damp, dark wilderness that Buck became enchanted by the rumors of a lost city, hidden for centuries by impenetrable forests south of the Amazon River. Though the mysterious city was known by many different names, Buck called it "Madeira."

"TO GET THROUGH THE FOREST, RISE ABOVE IT"

Returning to Baton Rouge in 1879, Buck turned his skills as a nautical engineer toward mastering the novel discipline of aeronautics. He believed a controlled airship was the best way to successfully explore the jungles that hid long-lost Madeira. Working alongside airship pioneers like Professor Peter Campbell, Charles Renard, and Paul Haenlein, Buck drew together plans for a cutting-edge airship—a paddleboat capable of traveling beyond the rivers, above the trees, and through the skies.

Timeline: APS Claire

1877 British surveyors mapping Brazil from a tethered balloon inspire Buck's navigable airship.

1879 Buck begins aeronautics study with fellow airship pioneers.

1882 Initial plans for the APS *Claire* are finalized. Buck begins construction of the lightweight gondola.

1885 Teaching aeronautics at the University of New Orleans, Buck meets future crewmembers Dr. Harriet Winchester and Chester Marone.

1886 Final tests on the envelope and ballonets. APS *Claire* deemed airworthy.

1887 APS *Claire*'s maiden voyage. Flies over Lake Pontchartrain, Baton Rouge, and New Orleans.

Foreword: The Fateful Expedition of 1889

THE JOURNEY BEGINS

In April 1888, Buck and his crew load APS *Claire* onto an ocean steamer bound for South America. After waiting out the rainy season, the *Claire* lifts off from Georgetown, British Guiana, on January 21, 1889, and slips over the tropical highlands and down into the Amazon basin. Flying with stiff tailwinds, the dirigible makes a record-shattering flight of nearly 1,500 miles in just ten days. The flight, while quick, is made treacherous by turbulence, storms, and numerous steep ravines.

TOWARD MADEIRA

After a lengthy delay in Iquitos, Peru, the *Claire* continues 800 miles southeast, exploring the western side of the Madeira River in search of the city. Enroute, a strong tropical storm thrashes the *Claire* for days. The crew rides out the fierce weather by anchoring to a tall tree and taking shifts at night stoking the boilers to keep the ship afloat. After the storm, the *Claire* limps north to Manaus, Brazil, where she makes port to fix structural damage to the gondola and envelope.

THE DISAPPEARANCE

The *Claire*'s next course takes her between the Madeira and Tapajós Rivers, one of the most remote places in the world. On August 19, 1889, Buck's distinctive airship is spotted nearly 350 miles up the Tapajós by the riverboat PS *Gilbert*. The Gilbert reports that the *Claire* signals, "city found south," before heading directly into an approaching storm front. The ship is never seen again.

IN SEARCH OF THE CLAIRE:

In 2009, we organized an expedition to retrace the flight course of APS *Claire*, hoping to find evidence of either Buck's journey or his lost city. For months, we navigated above the Amazon rainforest in a sturdy modern airship. Even so, despite every modern technological advantage, the trip was harrowing. We encountered sudden thunderstorms, massive fog-shrouded hills, and towering trees that jutted out of the forest like deadly pikes. Finally, in October 2009, we spotted a small trunk jettisoned from the *Claire* that had remained suspended 200 feet in the Amazonian canopy for over a century. In the trunk we found a compass, a watch, maps, several peculiar gold coins, and, most importantly, Buck's original drawings for his vanished ship, complete with handwritten notes about the expedition. It is this spectacular find that we share with you now.

Over the Paranatinga River in September 2009.

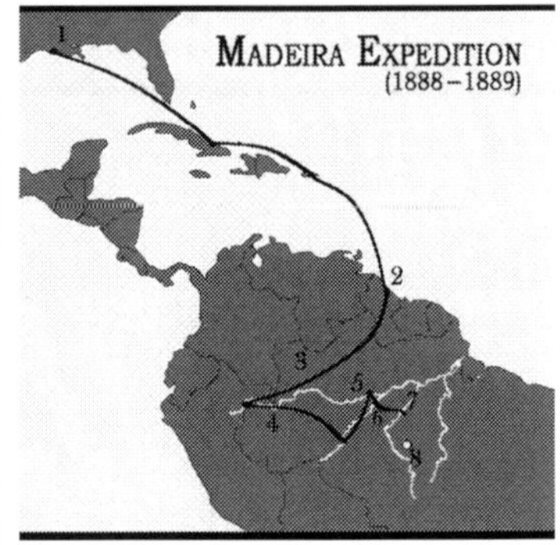

APRIL 1888
Departs New Orleans, U.S.

JULY 1888
Arrives Georgetown, British Guiana

JANUARY 21, 1889
Georgetown to Iquitos (1,500 miles in ten days)

JUNE 15, 1889
Departs Iquitos for Madeira River (near Porto Velho)

JUNE 30, 1889
Emergency landing in Manaus, Brazil

AUGUST 15, 1889
Course to Madeira and Tapajós Rivers

AUGUST 19, 1889
Final sighting by PS *Gilbert*

OCTOBER 2009
Trunk from APS *Claire* recovered

Schematic Illustrations for

Air Paddle Steamer Claire

patents pending 1887

Property of the J.T. Buck Airship Company

[CONFIDENTIAL MATERIALS ENCLOSED]

If found please return to—

J.T. Buck Airship Company
700 Canal Street
New Orleans, Louisiana
United States of America

Tethered observation balloon over the Xingu River.

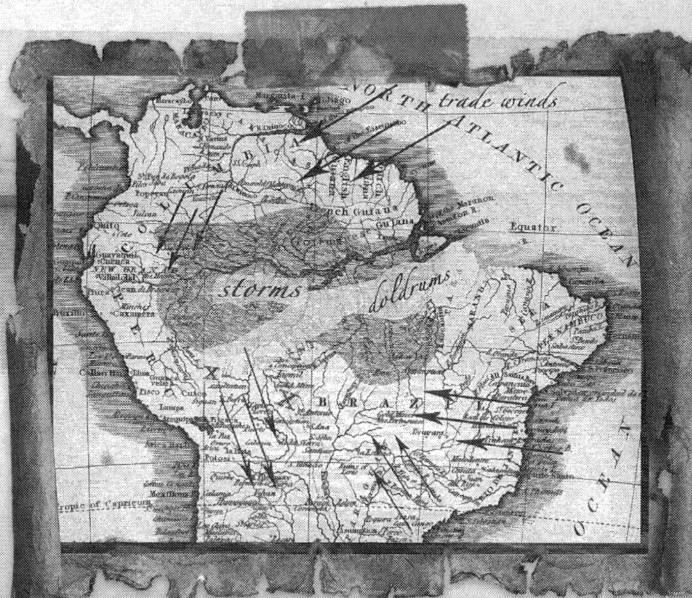

"Daguerreotype of Madeira" - Lt. J. Barnes, 1851

Madeira Is the Missing Piece

I believe this city we seek was the original spring of civilization from which the wondrous Inca, Maya, and Aztec civilizations descended. Like Athens, Babylon, and Rome, it has stood as a metropolis ahead of its time with perhaps 400,000 inhabitants—a great center of commerce and arts, with vast highways traversing the jungle. According to native lore, for many generations talented citizens built extraordinary towers and navigated the forest with ease and speed. Before Rome, they were inventors of fantastic technologies, perhaps having realized many of our modern gadgetries and advanced industries some thousands of years prior.

Alas, the jungle is all-consuming, capable of devouring magnificent civilizations in mere decades. Solving this mystery shall be the highlight of my very existence.

Crew of the APS Claire

Dr. Harriet Winchester

Age & Origin: 33 years old
New York, New York
Education: Doctor of Medicine; Served in New Mexico Territory during Lincoln County War
Duties Onboard: Doctor, Botanist
Notes: A fearless adventurer & talented surgeon. Lived seven years on the frontier. Shot twice while tending wounded in Lincoln County War. Also quite charming conversationalist and worthy chess opponent. Prone to airsickness.

Chester Marone

Age & Origin: 37 years old
Savannah, Georgia
Education: Master Engineer
Duties Onboard: Chief Engineer, Second Aviator, Navigator, Cook
Notes: Reliable, resiliant, and highly intelligent. First-rate captain, in air and at sea. Unquenchable thirst for high-risk adventure. Hot-tempered and quick to fight. As cook, food is generally unpalatable at best, inedible at worst.

Bachue Amaral

Age & Origin: 27 years old
Manaus, Brazil (Incan ancestry)
Education: Anthropologist
Duties Onboard: Translator, Hunter, Historian
Notes: Fluent in Portuguese, Spanish, Tupian, Arawakan, Pano-Takana. Mother is from Peru, father Indian of Brazil. Traveled to United States at 15. Highly educated. Very skilled hunter and quite handy with machete.

Takehiro Yoshimoto

Age & Origin: Unkown (around 50)
Hagi, Japan
San Francisco, California
Education: Samurai
Duties Onboard: Security & Defense, Hunting & Fishing, Head Explorer
Notes: Indisposable, brave, and fierce warrior. Also an expert fisherman and highly knowledgeable about forest flora & fauna. Sharp sense of humor. Calm in demeanor and natural leader in tense scenarios.

Parts of the A.P.S Claire

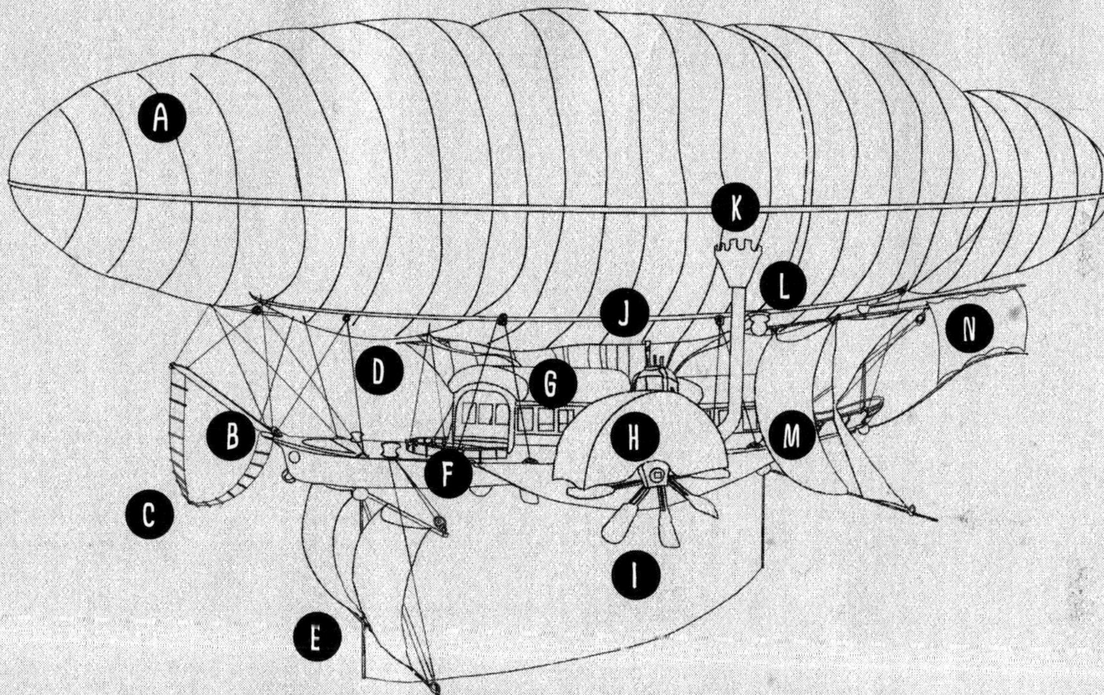

A. Envelope

B. Bowsprit

C. Gangplank/Ladder

D. Rigging

E. Foremast (square rig)

F. Hull

G. Crew cabin

H. Propeller guard

I. Paddle propeller

J. Boiler/Engine

K. Smokestack

L. Galley/Engineer's cabin

M. Mainsail

N. Rudder

Choosing the Design

Gondola Components

A. Crew cabin

B. Boiler

C. Galley/Engineer's cabin

D. Propeller guard

E. Propeller range

F. Main hull

G. Outrigger hull

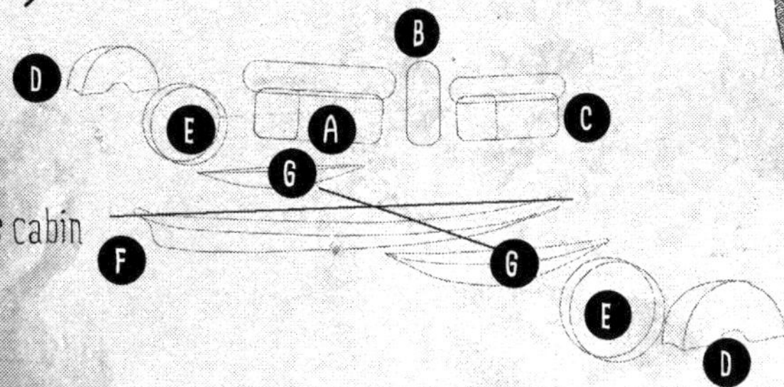

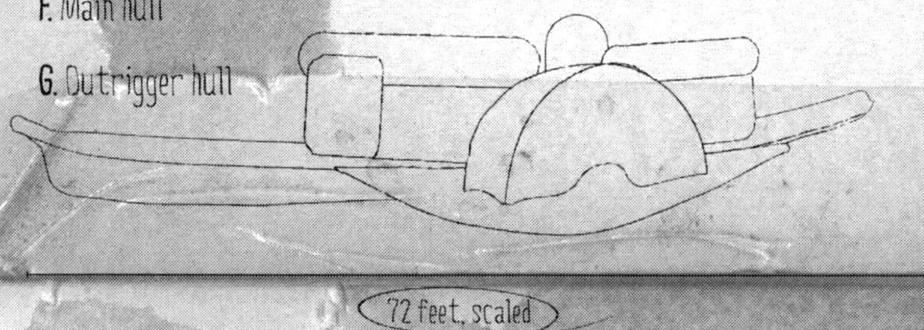

My original concept for the journey's vessel was this simple, open riverboat with two helium balloons, a small engine, and a single propeller that could carry two passengers about 100 miles in fair weather. When I realized the enormity of this expedition's undertaking, it was necessary to think larger.

Drawing the Gondola

Lightly sketch two crossing lines (scaled to 72 feet long). Draw the propeller guard as a semi circle in the lower-right quadrant. Beneath it, an elongated semicircle makes the outrigger hull. Atop the outrigger hull, two bread-loaf shaped cabins sit on either side of the ship's boiler (the smaller half-cylinder). Finally, add the boat's main hull with two gently curving lines that start at the bow and taper as they approach the rounded stern.

It was my design for a lightweight Mississippi paddleboat named **PS *Duke Charles*** that was inspiration for the ***Claire***.

Boilers and Lifting Gases

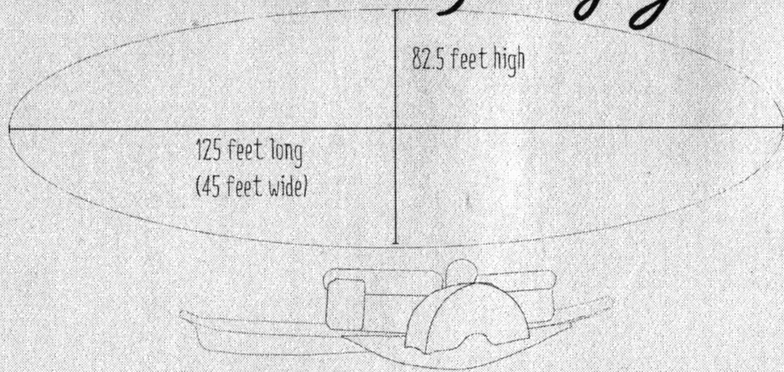

On this expedition, we are creating our own hydrogen lifting gases midflight! A Gramme Machine, installed in an external compartment, feeds electric current through water, which splits the molecules from H_2O into oxygen and hydrogen. The oxygen is expelled back into the boiler's firebox while the hydrogen is diverted into the ballonets for lift. In addition, heated air may be diverted from the boiler's exhaust for trim.

Sizing the Balloon

In order to achieve buoyancy, the balloon should be sized as an oval 125 feet long (shown scaled) by 82.5 feet high. The balloon should center over the hull's midpoint.

Piping

Piping from the Gramme Machine to ballonets.

A Multipurpose Boiler

Aside from powering the propellers and Gramme Machine, the boiler is also used to heat the galley oven and filter river water for drinking.

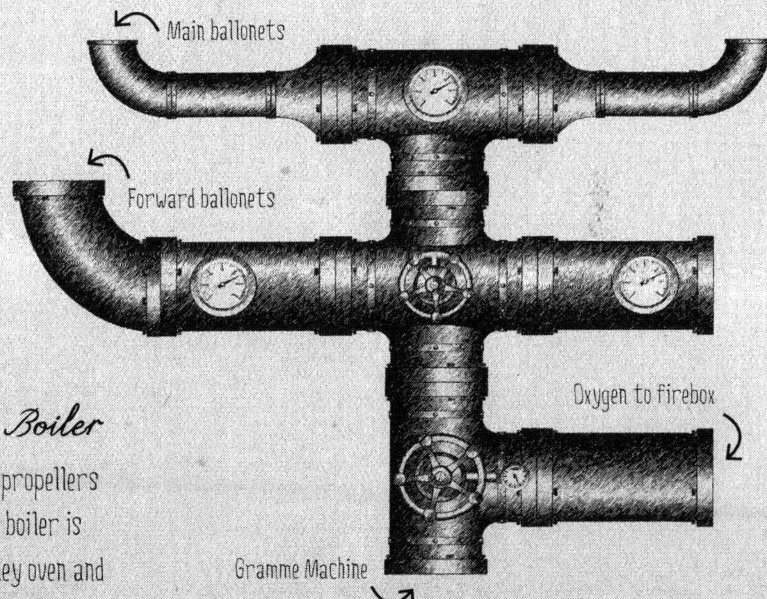

Ballonets

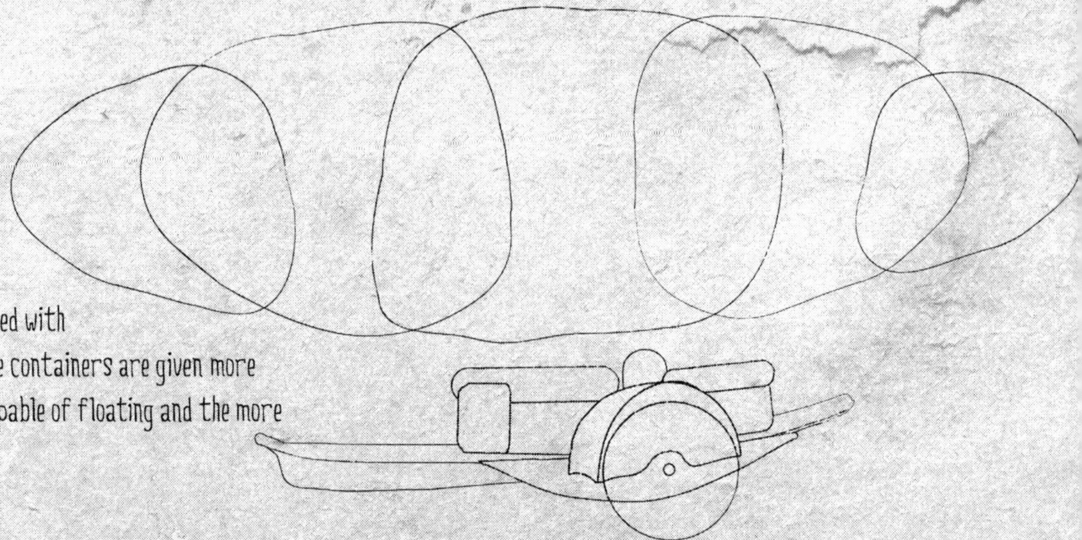

Achieving Buoyancy

Hydrogen gas is significantly lighter than the air in the atmosphere, allowing containers filled with hydrogen to float in midair. As these containers are given more hydrogen gas, the higher they are capable of floating and the more weight they are capable of lifting.

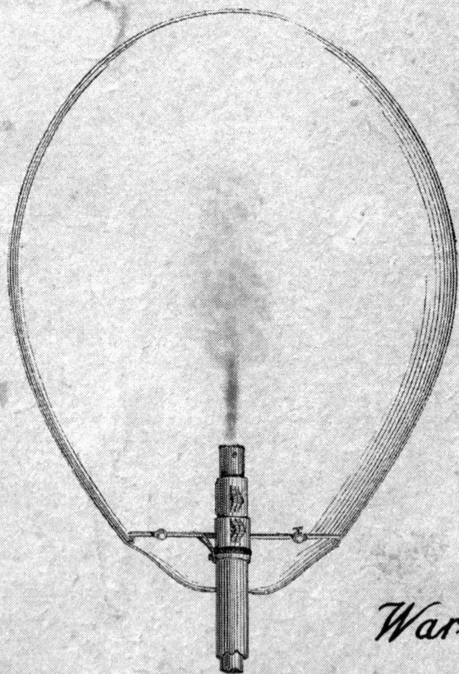

Envelope and Propeller Range

Reduce the balloon area to five overlapping compartments. These will make up the envelope (outer skin of the balloon) that will be stretched over a frame to protect the inner ballonets. Next, sketch the circular range of the propellers.

Ballonets

The airship is kept aloft by four separate ballonets (gasbags), evenly spaced along the envelope. Made of durable rubber, the fore and aft ballonets are the largest, and simply inflating or deflating one or the other controls the pitch of the ship. Since they are dangerously close to the boiler, the central ballonets are significantly smaller and only used for supplementary lift.

Warning: Hydrogen gas is extremely flammable.

Propellers

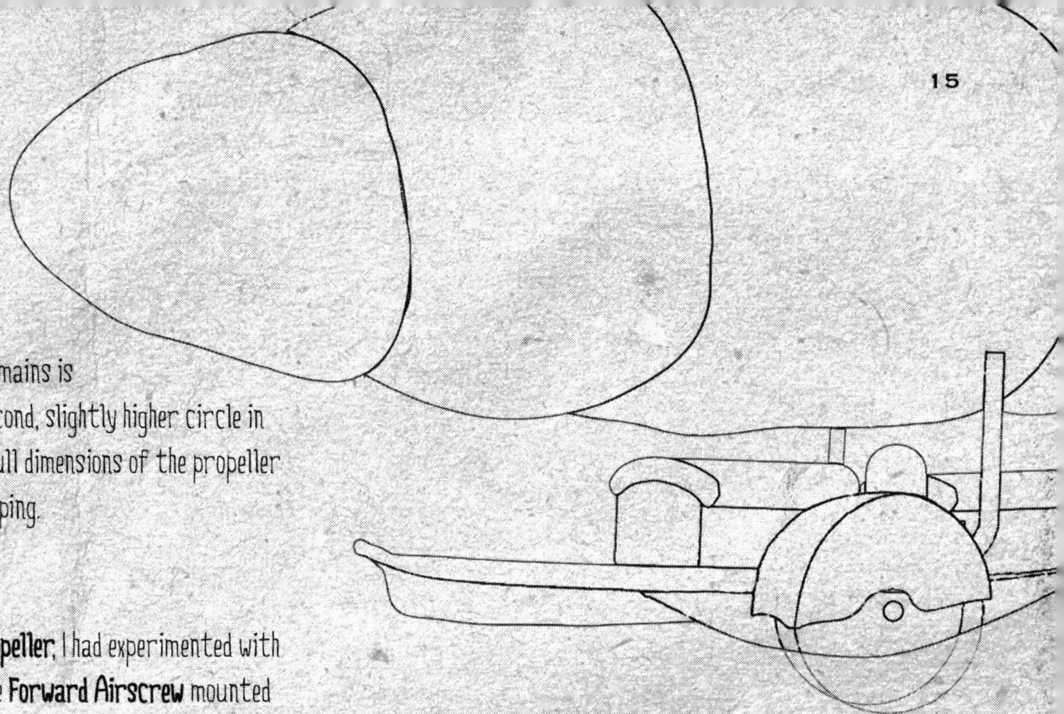

Outer Envelope and Propeller Dimensions

Eliminate the excess lines separating the ballonet compartments so that all that remains is a smooth, outer skin and its folds. Add a second, slightly higher circle in the propeller zone. This will determine the full dimensions of the propeller blades. Insert the smokestack and balloon piping.

Deciding on Propellers

Before realizing the power of the **Paddle Propeller**, I had experimented with a number of other options, including a single **Forward Airscrew** mounted on the front of the ship, **Dual-Beam Fan Propellers** that jutted out from either side of the hull, and **Envelope-Based Dual Propellers** on either side of the balloon itself. In the end, however, the Paddle Propellers allowed for the most speed and mobility.

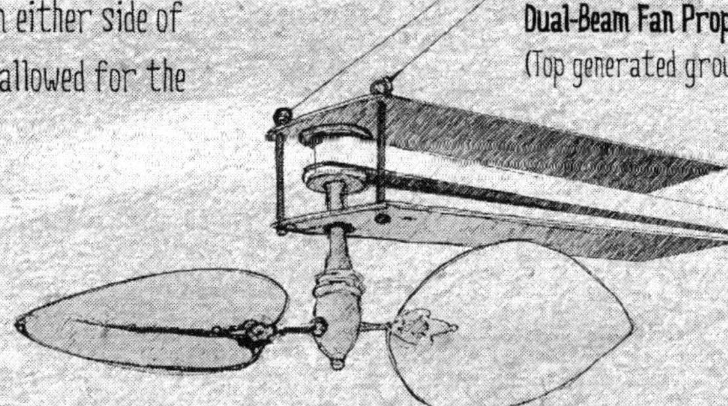

Dual-Beam Fan Propellers
(Top generated ground speed: 18 mph)

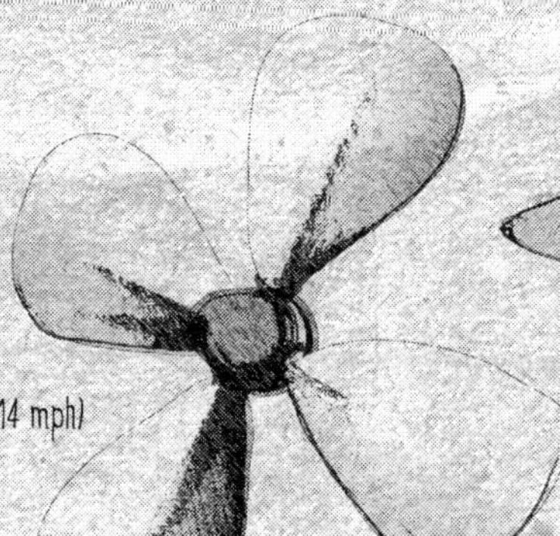

Forward Airscrew
(Top generated ground speed: 14 mph)

Envelope-Based Dual Propellers
(Top generated ground speed: 25 mph)

Dangers Above

We may not be traveling on the treacherous forest floor, but that does not mean that dangers are not everpresent.

In the Trees

Tree-dwelling **Poison Snakes** may slither up bow lines to find a safe place to rest.

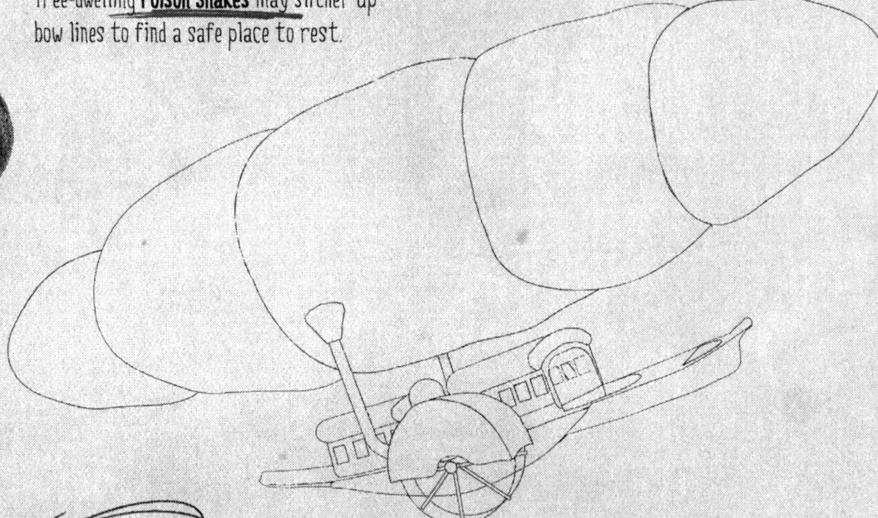

Monkeys will climb the anchor line to steal anything they can carry.

In the Air

Blood-sucking **Vampire Bats** patrol the jungle

Harpy Eagles are enormous, carnivorous, and ill-tempered

Drawing the Decks

Atop the hull, sketch in the cabin windows, companionway, cockpit, and gunwales. Add a stack cover to the smokestack to prevent sparks from igniting the hydrogen-filled ballonets. Draw in the propeller roots to look like spokes on a wheel.

Hunting and Collecting Water in the Amazon

To supplement our limited stores of dried goods, we will need to forage for food from the forest. Fortunately, plenty of hunting and picking options await under the rich canopies.

Tropical Fruits

Water collection can be done from 100 feet up with a motorized pulley.

Forward Ho!

It is time to attach those propeller blades! In addition, draw the base of the masts for the sails. Those propellers can use some wind-fed help.

River Creatures

Tambaqui and Catfish

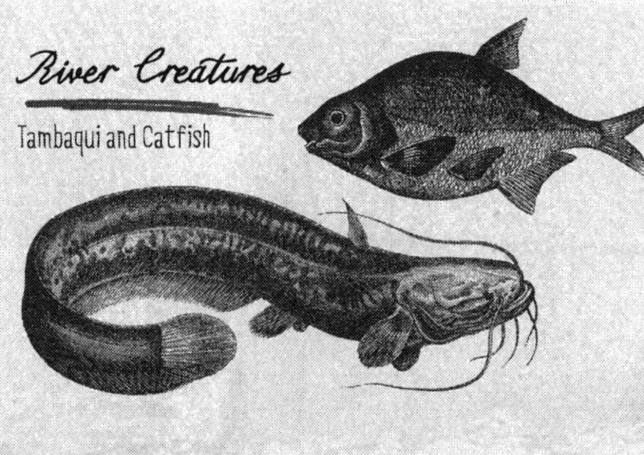

Land Beasts

Capybara, Giant Anteater, and Tapir

Alternate Observation Transports

High-Altitude Aerostat

One tank of oxygen and this lofty ballooner can take observations from nearly 25,000 feet!

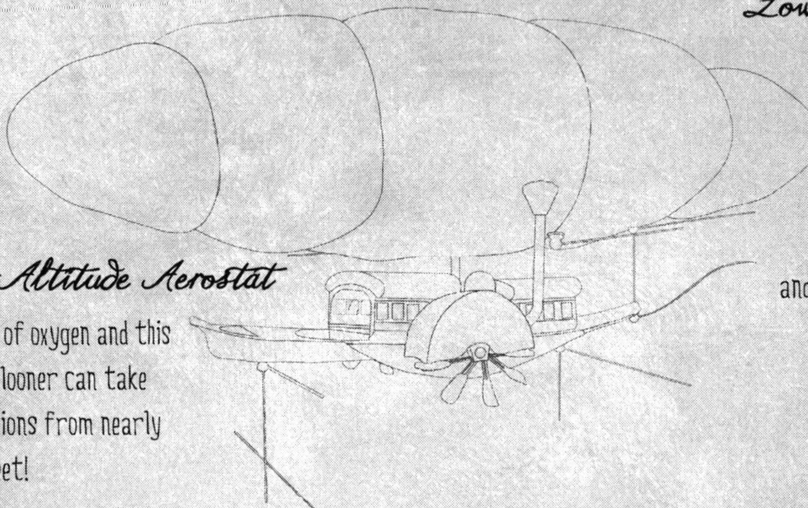

Lowering the Masts

The ship's control will be aided by three separate sail configurations: a square-rigged foremast, the mainsails, and an elegant rudder. Secure the masts and spars.

Lightweight Motorized Roaming Machine

This simple, steam-powered buggy makes exploring open lands quite enjoyable and speedy.

Both small riverboats and observation kites are packed on board. Here, a boat trails a kite through a waterway.

Forest Exploration

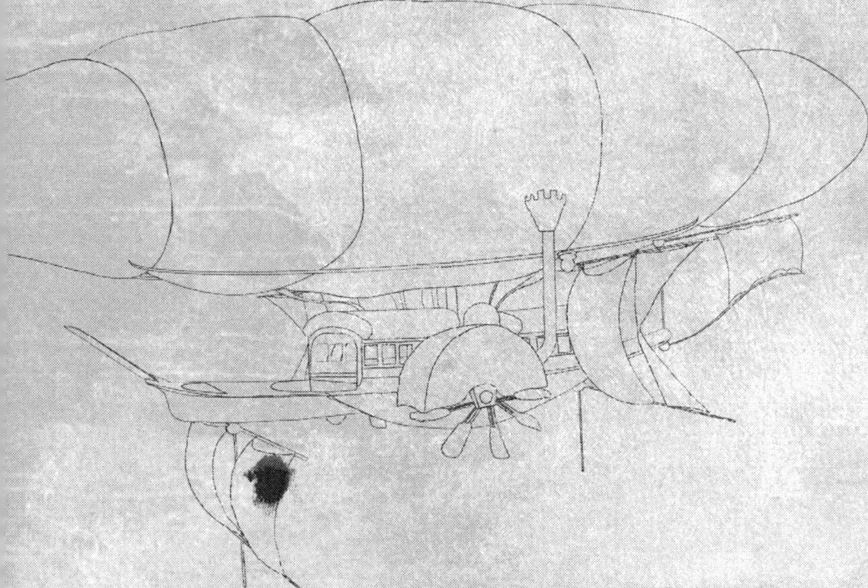

Venturing out on the forest floor is rarely safe. Day and night, plenty of predators hunt on land and in the water. Care must be taken at all times—travel in pairs and always bring a rifle or two. By all means, stay out of murky streams and pools.

Pumas (Cougars)

Electric Eels

Under Sail and Almost Under Way

Rig the sails to their respective spars and masts. Trim the outer-most mainsail by pinching it together in the middle. Remember, the farther out to stern the rudder is, the more effective it will be at turning the ship.

Piranha

Daily Schedule

0600-0610: (Sunrise) Anchor's aweigh; breakfast.
0630-0800: Fetch & filter daily water ration/fuel supply.
0800-0830: Morning meeting; weather observation; tasks assigned.
0845-1315: Travel (weather permitting).
1330: Luncheon.
1345 hrs-1600 hrs: Ground expeditions (various).
1630: All hands onboard. Evening surveying.
1645-1800: Travel.
1800-1810: (Sunset) Weigh anchor. First night shift begins.
1900 hrs: Supper.
1945-2100: Leisure time: chess, reading, tinkering, journaling.
2100 hrs: Lights out.
2100-2300: Second night shift.
2300-0100: Third night shift. Celestial observations.
0100-0300: Fourth night shift. Boiler check.
0300-0500: Fifth night shift.
0500-0600: Dawn shift.

Evening leisure time on board.

Observations are recorded into the ship's phonoautograph.

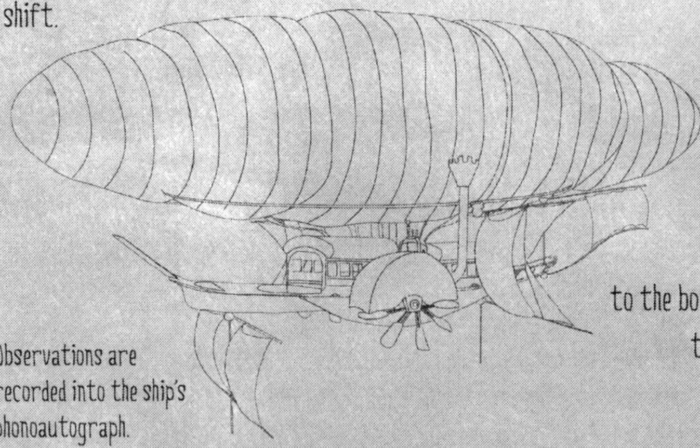

Lifting the Gondola

Install the vertical rigging on the outside of the envelope. This will allow for the even distribution of the gondola's weight. Add a few final touches to the boiler top and secure the pushpit railing at the ship's stern for the crew's protection.

Anchoring and Disembarking

Anchoring

Two types of anchoring are employed throughout the expedition. The most effective is traditional anchoring, which we may only weigh in open fields.

The second, and far more difficult, method is to lash the boat to the trunk of a tall tree (or trees). This is used only when no forest clearing can be found.

Descending and Ascending from the Deck

Disembarking (and returning to) the ship without stopping the ship's movement is challenging, but can be done. We've developed three methods: The Rope Descender, Forward Ladder, and the Hook & Eye Extractor, which allows explorers to be snatched aboard while transporting a heavy load.

Preparing to Descend

On the bow side of the ship, draw in the pulpit railing, and deck fittings (the chocks and cleats used to tie up the ship). Add a ladder to the gangplank so the crew can reach the ground while the airship is still afloat.

Ropes, Rigging, and Sailing

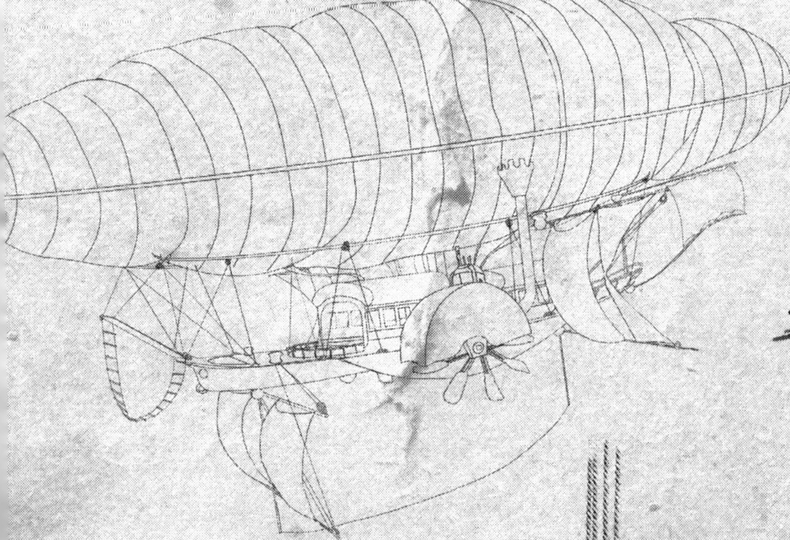

Rigging the Gondola to the Balloon

Officially marry the balloon and gondola by lashing them together from bow to stern. Make sure your ropes form a series of triangles (the strongest shape) to maximize stability in the air.

Knots

A. Overhand
B. Double figure eight
C. Square
D. Overhand bow

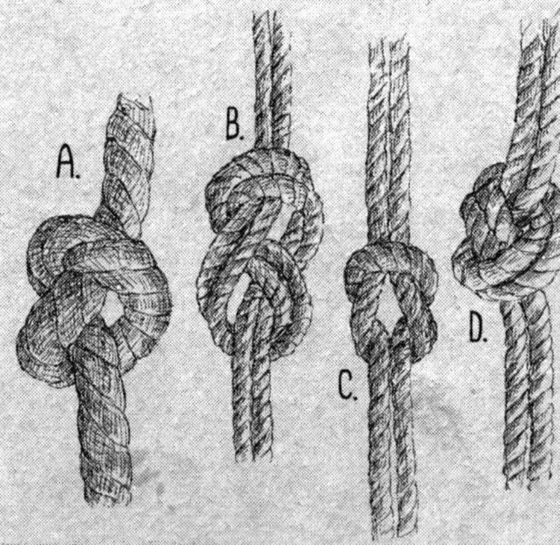

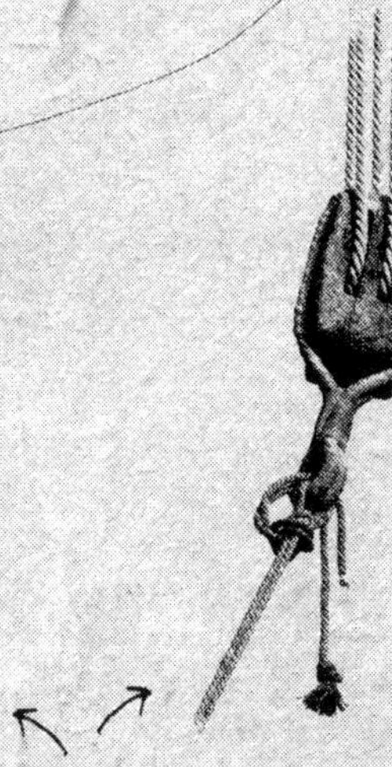

Lightweight block and tackle make it easier to lift heavy loads as well as steer the ship.

Proper sailing techniques can make for very fast airships. Here are the plans for the **Portuguese Bahia Air Racer**, a powerless airship capable of traveling almost 120 mph!

Expedition Artifacts

Near the Madeira River, we came across numerous coins from ages past.

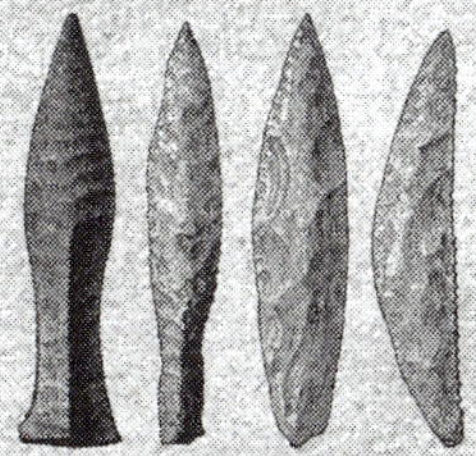

Thousands of carefully crafted arrowheads litter the forest floor.

Spectacular Finds on the Forest Floor

Midway through the expedition, just south of the Amazon River, we began finding numerous artifacts of interest. Among the most surprising finds-about two dozen gold coins from around the world, not only from the Inca, Aztec, and Spanish, but coins that appear to have been from ancient Rome and Greece. Could this lost city be the Atlantis of lore?

An ancient rock carving depicting a staggeringly modern-looking city.

Shadow and Light

Begin by adding the cross rigging to the top of the envelope. Then choose a light source and sketch the initial elements of shadow and light. The hull of the ship, facing groundward, should be darkened significantly, along with the stern of the ship, hidden beneath the balloon.

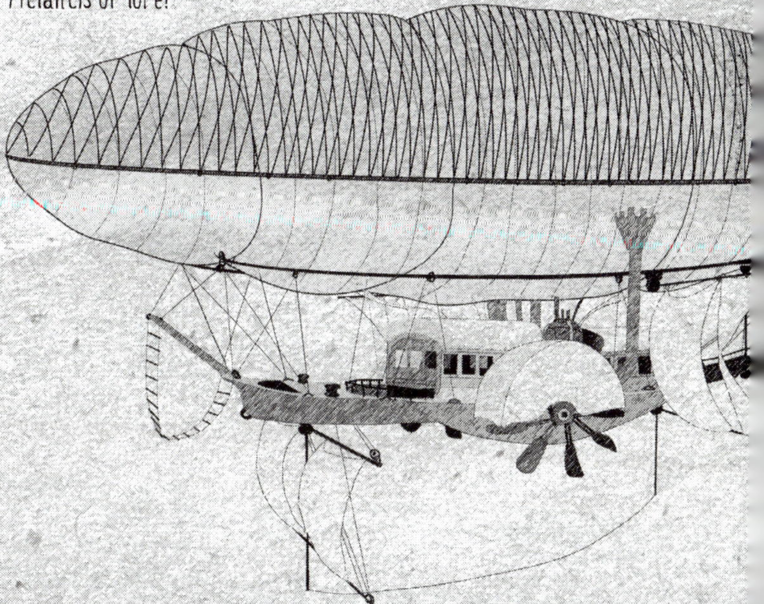

Communicating with the Outside World

Electromagnetized Messenger Crafts

Communicating with the civilized world will be vital to this expedition. At first, I considered homing pigeons but they are too vulnerable to Amazon's aerial predators. Instead, I designed and hand-launched ten coal-powered crafts—lightweight, speedy, and capable of transporting up to three sizeable letters in a sealed box. The navigator bulb is drawn, much like the needle of a compass, to electromagnetic waves emanating from a transmagomitter tower in Iquitos. The range of flight is approximately 750 miles.

Adding Balloon Dimension

Continue to shade the balloon and gondola. Bring out the round shapes of the balloon by shading the folds, bottom, and a bit on top. In this image, the light source is directly behind the viewer. Next, darken some of the shadows on the gondola, including making the crew cabin a nice, cool place to escape to.

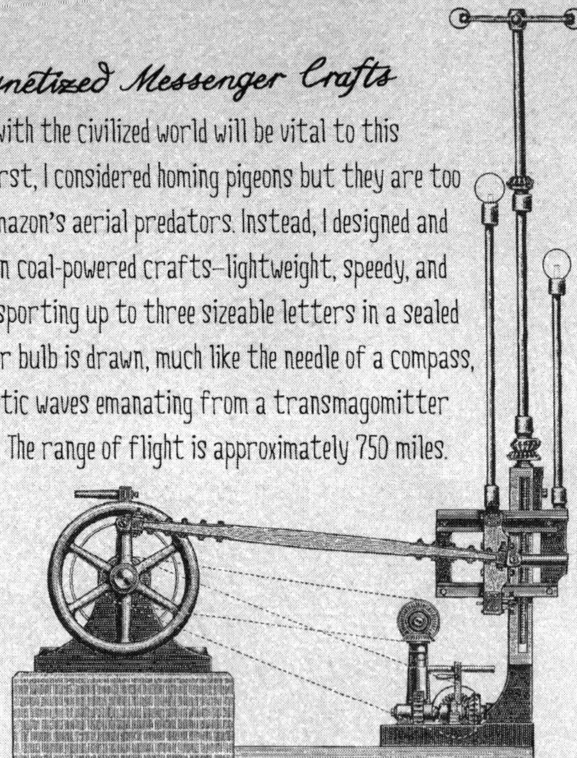

Fixed Transmagomitter

Ship-Launched
Messenger Craft

Storms and Thunderheads

The Final Step

Before taking to the skies, add a couple personal flourishes to the ship. Perhaps a company logo or some elegant design. Then start up the boiler, stoke the fire, and give the engine a test.Add that smoke coming out of the stack.

Left: An innocent-looking cloud now can turn into a nasty thunderstorm in mere hours.

Navigating Bad Weather

High winds may blow an airship off course, but a thunderstorm can wreak havoc. Unfortunately, the Amazon Basin is known for severe weather. The hot and humid forest itself can produce its own clouds through evaporation. When enough clouds are produced they can gather into immense thunderstorms. The greatest danger of these storm systems are their powerful updrafts and downdrafts. A single thunderhead can suck an airship from an elevation of 1,000 feet to 10,000 feet in a matter of seconds. And downdrafts can bring those trees below a whole lot closer. During the expedition, we'll steer as far clear of any storm systems as possible. With our speed, we should be able to get around most of them.

This airship was sucked into a storm cloud by a strong updraft.

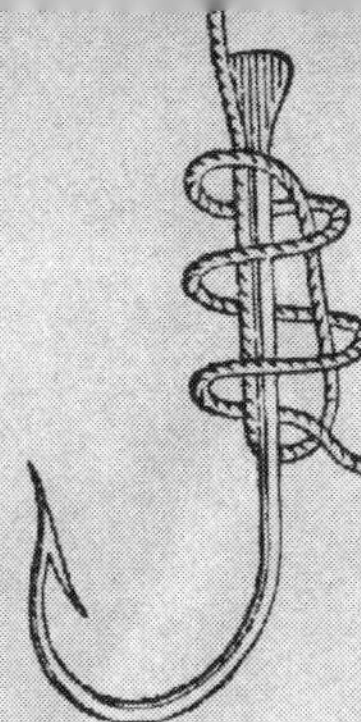

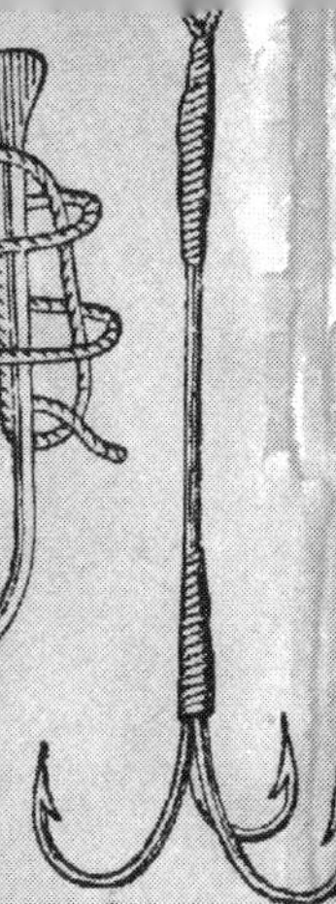

Components, Equipment, & Ship's Log

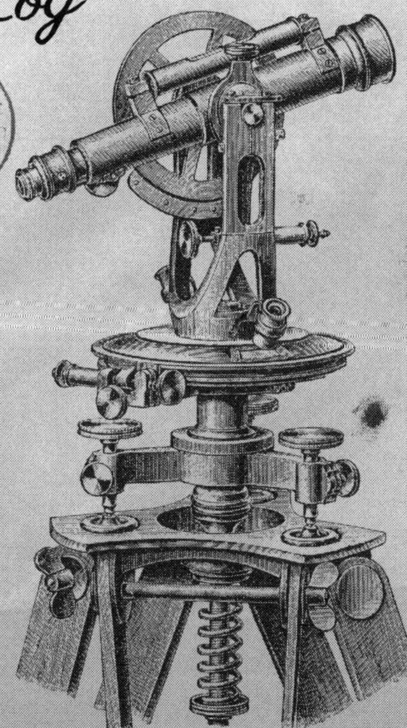

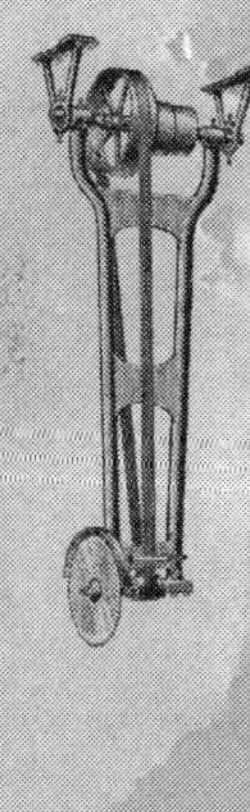

Equipment List

Hunting and Exploring

Firearms:
Rifles
Pistols
Shotguns
Harpoon guns

Fishing:
Poles
Lines
Hooks
Nets

Blades:
Swords
Hatchets
Hunting knives
Axes

Explosives:
Dynamite
Flares

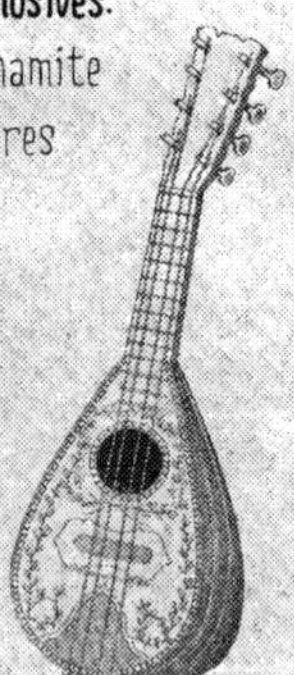

Navigatory

Anemometer
Weatherometer
Compasses
Sextants
Maps
Timepieces
Difference engine
Elevatimitter

Observations

Telescope (fixed to hull of ship)
Paper strip photographic film
Optical theodolites
Monoculars
Ooglometer
Binoculars
Camera
Periscope
Depthobarometer

Crew

Goggles
Flight caps
Weather insulators
Typewriter
Chess Set
Cards
Banjo
Mandolin
Harmonica
Harpismonium
Airsickness tablets
Antifogmatics
Medical supplies & kits
Wound salves
Expedition travel sacks

Engines and Engineering

Portable boiler
Gramme machine
Automated hauling device
Boiler sealant
Engineering repair kits
Automated cutting device
Welder's torch
Leather smocks
Spare ballonets
Envelope patches
Fire extinguisher
Spare bolts, flanges, fasteners, and gears
Spars
Tool kits
Vulcanized rubber
Rope

Communications

Phonoautograph
Miniature magnetic
Messenger machines
Megaphonifier
Stationery
Ground-locating flares

Additional Transports

High-altitude aerostat
Roaming machine
Observation kites
Observation balloons

Alternate Propeller Designs

Forward Airscrew

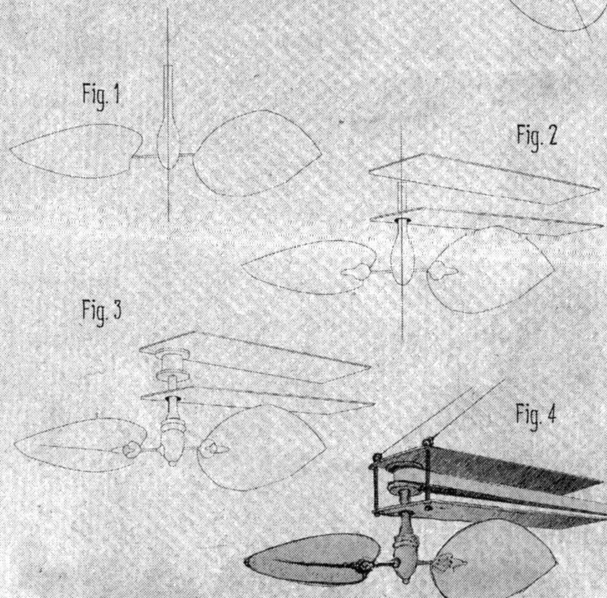

Beam-Fan Propeller

Envelope-Based Dual Propeller

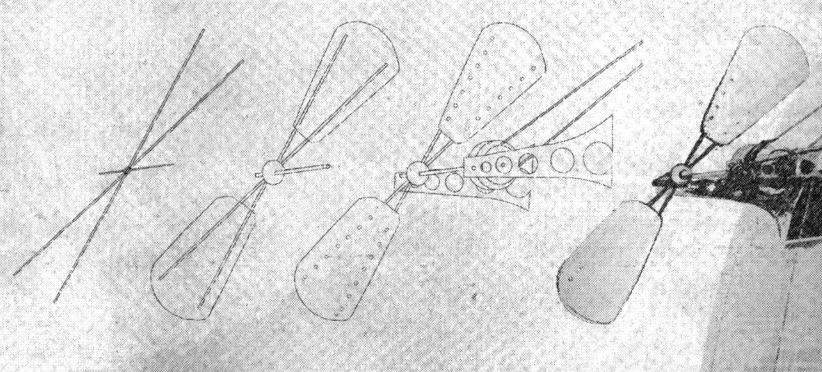

Ship's Steam Engine and Portable Boiler

I've perfected this two-compartment boiler. Lower compartment is the firebox, water tank above. Excess steam and smoke escape through the stacks on top.

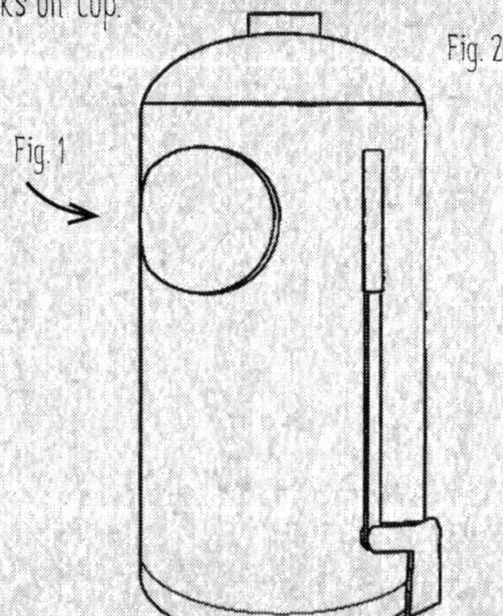

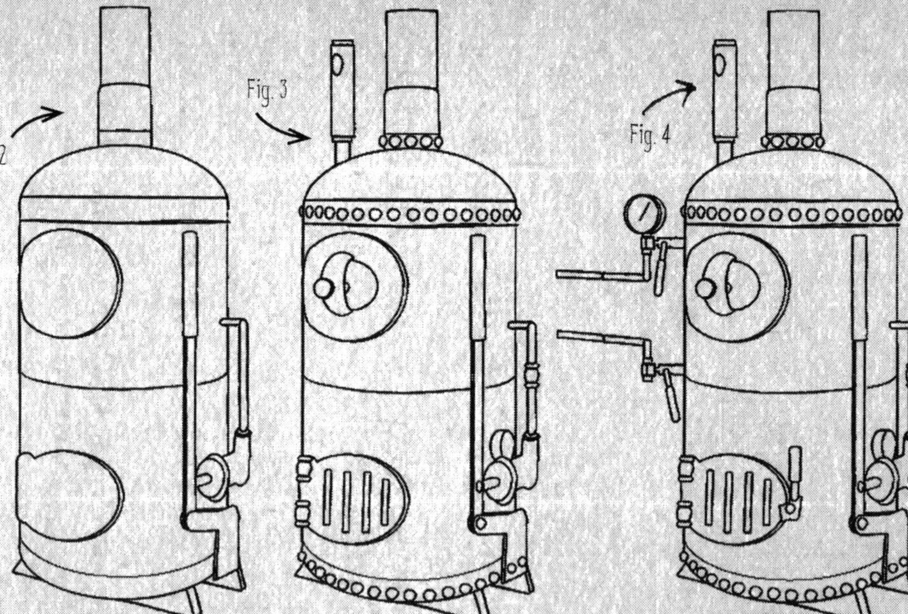

This portable boiler can be hooked up to all sorts of additional transports such as the High-Altitude Aerostat or Roaming Machine. In emergency situations, it can also power the Gramme Machine to produce hydrogen.

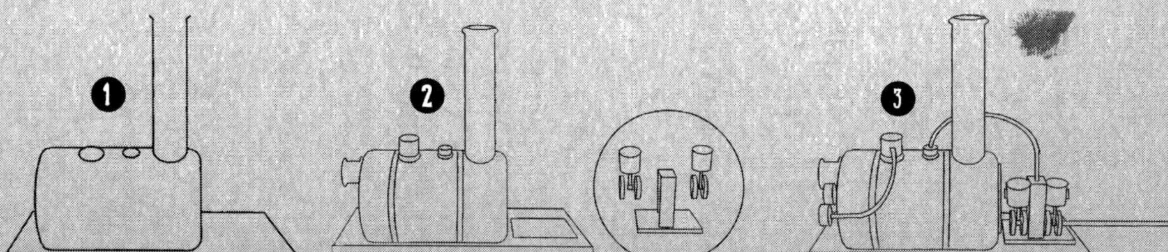

Gears, Gauges, and Levers

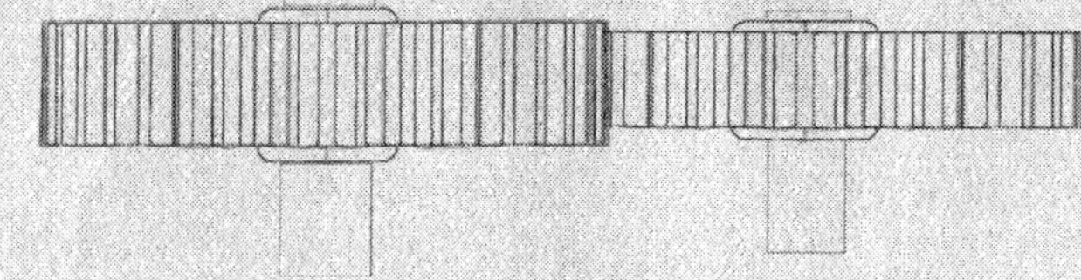

Meshing Spur Gears

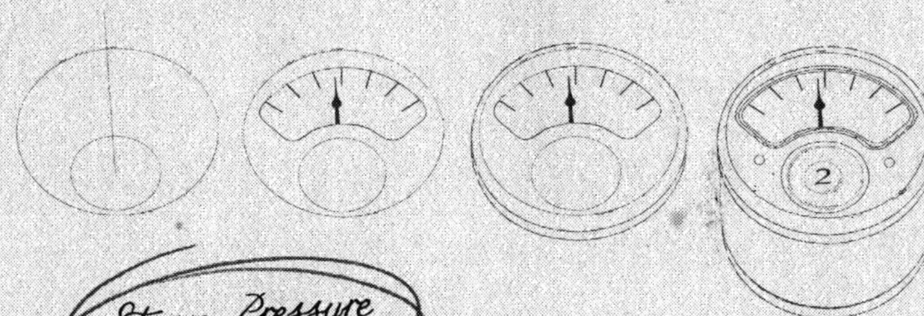

Steam Pressure Gauge

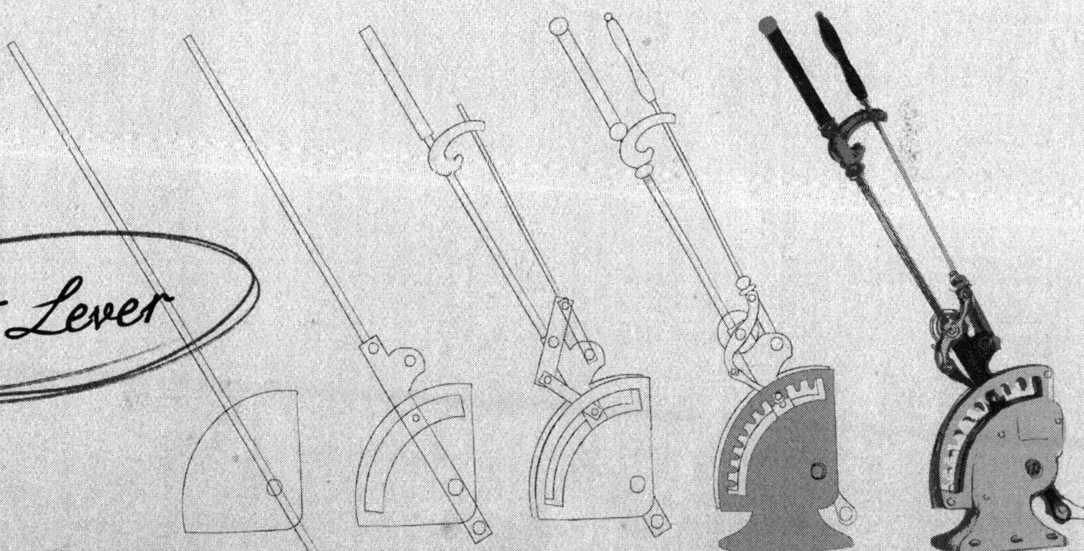

Thrust Lever

Claire's Ship Log

Jan. 20: Final preparations made. Departure tomorrow at 0500. Scattered rains tonight—tapering off.

Jan. 21: Clear skies for a successful launch! Making good time over Guiana Highlands. Following Essequibo River. Made nearly 250 miles (approx) with stiff tailwind.

Jan. 23: Another 200 miles east-southeast today. In Brazil now. Steep ravines making low flying treacherous. Inflated ballonets to cruise at 1,000 feet but air very turbulent.

Jan. 25: Crossed over Branco and Negro Rivers just after sunrise. Two attempts to haul water from rivers midflight failed. Chester came within inches of falling overboard. Sweltering heat. Storms clouds on horizon. Made 130 miles.

Jan. 26: Storms all day! Heavy winds and rains. Secured ship to two trees but still took thrashing. Takehiro and Bachue hunted. Collected fuel/water. 0 miles today.

Jan. 27: Takehiro discovered 6' green boa constrictor coiled in the galley! It rode out the storm with us! Took the whole crew to release into the canopy. 250 miles.

Jan. 31: Made port in Iquitos. Crew granted land leave for 14 days. Harriet quite ill with malarial symptoms.

Feb. 4: Successful test of messenger crafts and transmagomitter for mail delivery.

Feb. 10: Disaster! The boiler thrunge plate cracked. Weeks to repair with rainy season ahead. Devastating.

Jun. 15: Finally back in the air. Enroute to Madeira River. 100 miles today.

Jun. 25: Massive storm tore hole in envelope the size of a piano. Ballonets exposed. Propellers damaged. No sign of city, making for Manaus. Outlook is grim.

Jun. 30: Safe landing in Manaus. Repairs.

Aug. 15: Back underway. Left Manaus. Bachue bartered 3 lbs capybara and 2 lbs dried river fish.

Aug. 16: Discoveries! Takehiro and Bachue found odd gold coins and rock carvings while on ground excursion. Coins appear ancient Roman/Greek?

Aug. 18: Forest getting denser, richer, eerie. Thick cloud forests. Harriet on obs. duty spotted a white the glimmer of...glass windows? Buildings? Possible? Vision quickly enveloped by spectacular, enormous storm front– 200 miles long. Treacherous flying. Evasive backtrack up Tapajos River.

Aug. 19: Crash. All hands alive but *Claire* wrecked. Packing equip. and departing on foot.

Wreckage of *Claire*. Discovered impressive rope bridge. Population close by?

The Fate of the Claire

Mnja Anjmna,

Ro hxd jan jkun cx mnlryqna cqrb vnbbjpn, yunjbn bnwm fxam cx vh fron, Lujran, cqjc R jv jc cqn oxuuxfrwp uxljcrxw: 7B 22', 61F 30'. R jv Sxwjcqjw C. Kdlt, jwm vh lanf jwm R qjen uxljcnm cqn panjc lrch xo Vjmnraj. Cqn lrch rb dwurtn jwh xcqna frcq cxfnarwp kdrumrwpb jwm kdbcurwp bcanncb. Rc rb caduh cqarerwp. Cqn rwqjkrcjwcb jan enah trwm jwm rwcnuurpnwc kdc qjen mnvjwmnm cqjc fn wxc cx unjen—wx oxanrpwna ljw orwm cqn lrch. Cqnh qjen bnnw cqn oxanbc jaxdwm cqn lrch mnbcaxhnm jwm mx wxc fjwc cx vnnc cqjc ojcn. R ljwwxc bjh R mrbjpann frcq cqnv.

Qnan jan cqn wjvnb xo vh lanf jwm cqnra ojcnb. Yunjbn pnc fxam cx cqnra ojvruh.

Ma. Qjaarnc Frwlqnbcna qjb sdvynm qnjmbcaxwp rwcx uxlju uron, unjawrwp jkxdc vnmrlrwju yujwcb jwm cnjlqrwp cqn qnjunab xo qna xfw vxmnaw vnmrlrwn. Bqn rb qjyyh.

Lqnbcna Vjaxwn qjb wnena knnw qjyyrna. Qn qjb cjtnw j fron jwm lujrvb qn rb orwrbqnm frcq jmenwcdan. Qn fruu xdc qrb uron rw cqrb lrch.

Kjlqdn Jvjaju uxwpb cx ancdaw cx qna ojvruh kdc bqn twxfb qna jwcqaxyxuxph anbnjalq qnan qjb knnw rwejudjkun.

Cjtnqrax Hxbqrvxcx qjb jbbrvrujcnm cx wjcren uron jwm rb xwn xo cqn eruujpn'b vxbc anbynlcnm qdwcnab.

Bqxdum hxd lqxxbn cx oxuuxf db rwcx cqn sdwpun, kn oxanfjawnm, cqn sxdawnh rb canjlqnaxdb. Kdc rc rb cqn jmenwcdan xo j uroncrvn.

Brwlnanuh,

J. T. Buck

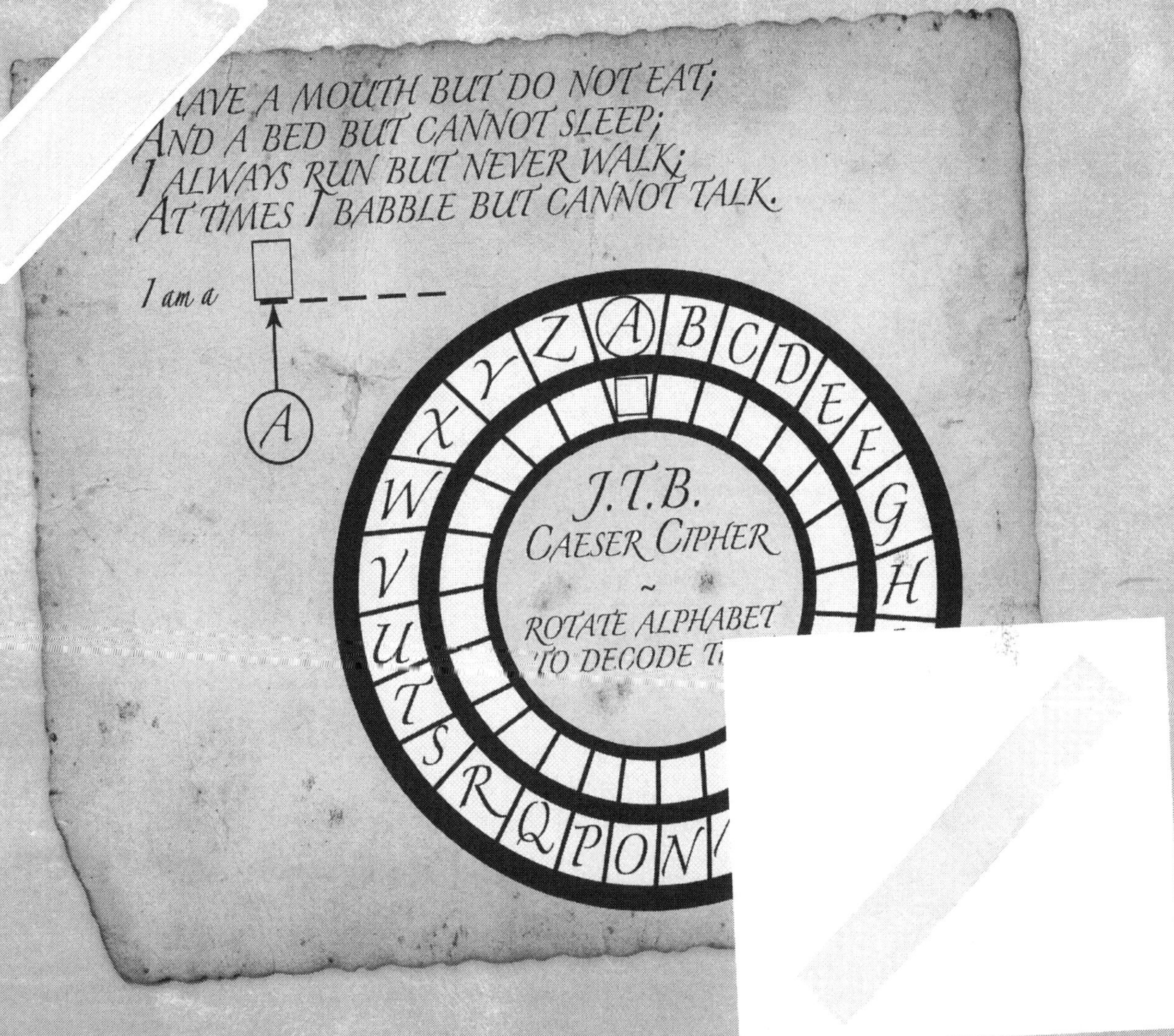
HAVE A MOUTH BUT DO NOT EAT;
AND A BED BUT CANNOT SLEEP;
I ALWAYS RUN BUT NEVER WALK;
AT TIMES I BABBLE BUT CANNOT TALK.
I am a
A
Z
A
B
C
D
E
F
G
H
W
V
U
T
S
R
Q
P
O
N
X
Y
J.T.B.
CAESER CIPHER
~
ROTATE ALPHABET
TO DECODE TH

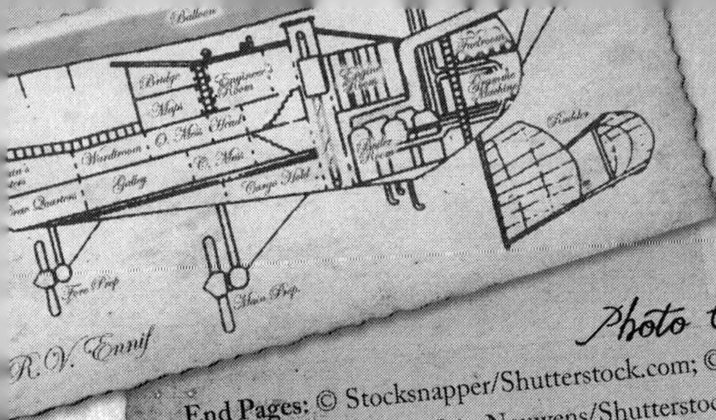

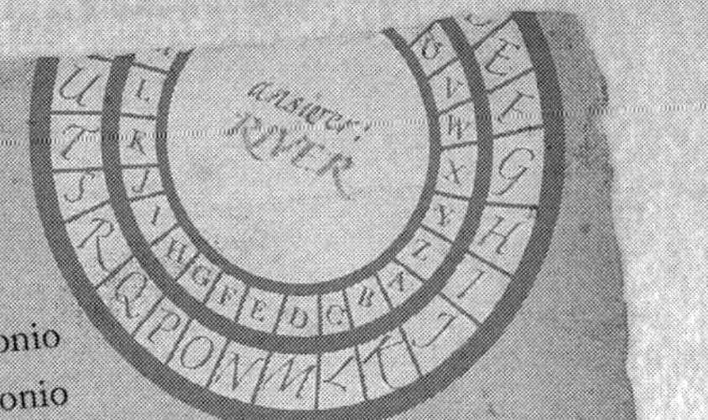

Photo Credits

End Pages: © Stocksnapper/Shutterstock.com; © Morphart Creations/Shutterstock.com; © Dover Publishing; © Hein Nouwens/Shutterstock.com; © AKaiser/Shutterstock.com; © Antonio Abrignani/Shutterstock.com. **Page 1:** © Jonathan Buck; © AKaiser/Shutterstock.com; © Antonio Abrignani/Shutterstock.com. **Page 2:** © Jonathan Buck; © Dover Publishing. **Page 3:** © SSSCCC/Shutterstock.com; © Dr. Morley Read/Shutterstock.com; © Cobalt88/Shutterstock.com. **Page 4:** © Antonio Abrignani/Shutterstock.com. **Page 5:** © Jonathan Buck. **Page 6:** © Antonio Abrignani/Shutterstock.com. **Page 7:** © Antonio Abrignani/Shutterstock.com; © Stephane Bidouze/Shutterstock.com; © Bertrand Benoit/Shutterstock.com; © Steven Wright/Shutterstock.com. **Page 8:** © Antonio Abrignani/Shutterstock.com; © Dover Publishing. **Page 9:** © Jonathan Buck. **Page 10:** © Jonathan Buck; © Dover Publishing; © Nicku/Shutterstock.com. **Page 11:** © Jonathan Buck; © PILart/Shutterstock.com. **Page 12:** © Jonathan Buck; © Antonio Abrignani/Shutterstock.com. **Page 13:** © Jonathan Buck. **Page 14:** © Jonathan Buck; © Hein Nouwens/Shutterstock.com. **Page 15:** © Jonathan Buck; © Guentermanaus/Shutterstock.com; © Artspace/Shutterstock.com; © Morphart Creations Inc./Shutterstock.com; © Hein Nouwens/Shutterstock.com. **Page 16:** © Jonathan Buck; © Dover publishing; © Antonio Abrignani/Shutterstock.com; © Hein Nouwens/Shutterstock.com. **Page 17:** © Jonathan Buck; © Hein Nouwens/Shutterstock.com; © Denis Barbulat/Shutterstock.com. **Page 18:** © Jonathan Buck; © Dr. Morley Read/Shutterstock.com; © Dover Publishing. **Page 19:** © Jonathan Buck; © Lantapix/Shutterstock.com; © Mansiliya Yury/Shutterstock.com; © Hein Nouwens/Shutterstock.com. **Page 20:** © Jonathan Buck; © Anki Hoglund/Shutterstock.com; © Nanisimova/Shutterstock.com; © Chronicler/Shutterstock.com; © Hein Nouwens/Shutterstock.com. **Page 21:** © Jonathan Buck; © Alessandro0770/Shutterstock.com; © Hein Nouwens/Shutterstock.com; © Morphart Creations Inc./Shutterstock.com. **Page 22:** © Jonathan Buck; © Hein Nouwens/Shutterstock.com; © AKaiser/Shutterstock.com. Page 23: © Jonathan Buck; © DSdesign/Shutterstock.com; © IgorGoloviniov/Shutterstock.com; © Antonio Abrignani/Shutterstock.com. **Page 24:** © Jonathan Buck; © Slava Gerj/Shutterstock.com. **Page 25:** © Hein Nouwens/Shutterstock.com. **Page 26:** © Hein Nouwens/Shutterstock.com; © Morphart Creations Inc./Shutterstock.com. **Page 27:** © Jonathan Buck. **Page 28:** © Jonathan Buck. **Page 29:** © Jonathan Buck. **Page 30:** © Mattalia/Shutterstock.com; © Bertrand Benoit/Shutterstock.com; © Mihai-Bogdan Lazar/Shutterstock.com; © Zastol'skiy Victor Leonidovich/Shutterstock.com. **Page 31:** © Keith Riegert. **Page 32:** © Keith Riegert.

FIRST
STEAM-PO
SOARING APP.
Wallace Soaring Machine
CA
DISCOVER
THE
W
IRWIN BROS.
GEARS
KNOBS
Barnes Steam Machines
B

NOVELTY AIR SHIP COMPANY
LIGHTER THAN AI AEROSTATS
UR THE VANISHING WILD WEST FROM
alifornia Airship Com
ly voyages depart SAN FRANC
s of the surrounding wilds an
ONTRA COSTA, before a
AKLAND adjacent the Fe
ice begins in June & continue
For voyage particulars and
CALIFORNIA AIRSHIP C
Market Street, S
New York
Brooklyn

Made in the USA
Columbia, SC
07 November 2021

48483127R00024